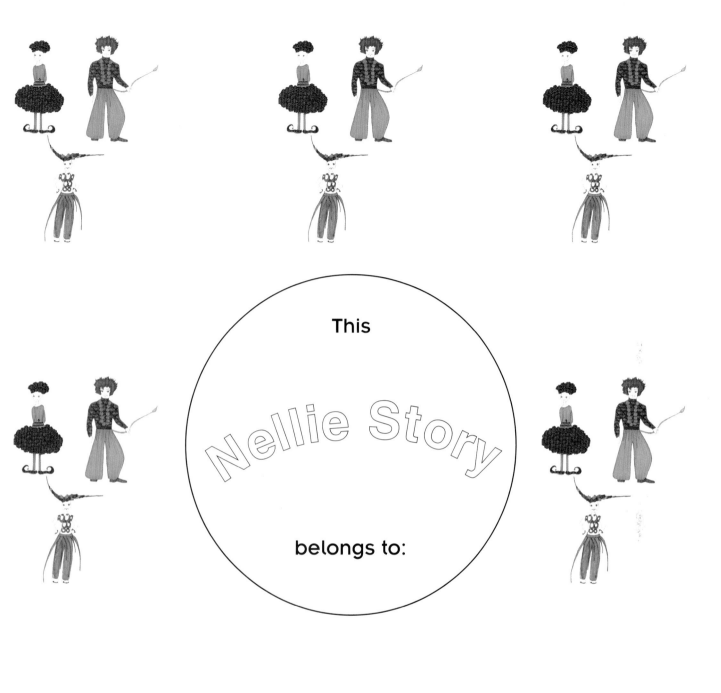

This

Nellie Story

belongs to:

_____

Dedicated to the peacemakers.

"There is no fear in love; but perfect love
casteth out fear..."
I John 4:18 (KJV)

Nellie Jelly and the Jelly Well © 2000 is about overcoming our foolish fears and prideful prejudices.

Text and Illustrations copyright © 2000 by Tamela Fleetwood

ISBN 0-970212-8-0-1
Library of Congress Catalog Card Number: 00-105756
Library of Congress Cataloging-in-Publication Data is available

Manufactured in Hong Kong
First Edition

Published by:
Odditeas, Inc. • 25 Palmetto Beach Drive • Post Office Box 1155 • Bluffton, South Carolina 29910
www.nelliejelly.com
www.odditeas.com

Nellie Jelly and the Jelly Well

Tamela Fleetwood

Once upon a jelly-jam day,
In a peaceful land so far away,
Where jelly jar trees can always be found,
And jelly-jam streams flow under the ground,
There once was a cook, whose name was Nellie,
And Nell was best known for jam and jelly.

"Jam days and jelly nights," they said.
"Very good on crackers or bread."

Nellie Jelly could claim her fame,
In the month of May when Nellie came,
To this live-for-today and let-it-be land,
Where jelly goop is in demand.
Nellie's jelly is truly best,
Much, much better than all the rest.

"Jam days and jelly nights," they said.
"Very good on crackers or bread."

One day dear sweet Nellie fell,

Down, down, down in a jelly-jam well.

Scared, and bruised, and scratched, and wet,

Not too worried...at least not yet.

The people heard her yell and shout.

She yelled, "Help!" and "Get me out!"

"Jam days and jelly nights," they said.

"Throw her a rope, or she'll be dead."

Nellie's hands were slicker than slick,

And to that rope they would not stick.

Nellie Jelly was out of luck.

She was very, very, very stuck.

Her friends did their best; they really tried.

"Oh no!" and "What'll we do?" they cried.

"Jam days and jelly nights," they said.

"Very good on crackers and bread."

Nellie said, "I think there's a way.
Don't worry please. I'll be okay.
We can make my slippery hands stick.
If we make this jelly goop thick.
Hmmm. Let me see, now let me think,
Go to the cupboard, next to my sink."

"Jam days and jelly nights," they said.
"Very good on crackers or bread."

They brought poor Nellie all of the spices,
Poured in the beans, the flour and the rices,
Added salt, and sugar and gel,
All in the hope of saving their Nell.
Nellie mixed, and mixed, and mixed, and mixed it.
Her friends cried out, "We hope you've fixed it!"

"Jam days and jelly nights," they said.
"Very good on crackers or bread."

Nellie Jelly began to cry.
The moon would soon be very high.
And, then the Jelly Monster slinks,
To jelly wells - for evening drinks.
But, what if, oh no! what if he,
Slurped her up, just like 1 - 2 - 3?

"Jam days and jelly nights," they said.
"Someone please call Mean Lady Red."

Lady Red was supposed to be,

Mean as wet e - lec - tri - ci - ty,

They said she could spit fire and sparks,

And, when she talks - she sort of barks.

But, she was Nellie's only chance.

'Cause when she played the monster danced.

"Jam days and jelly nights," they said.

"Very good on crackers or bread."

They begged, and screamed, and yelled, and cried.

"Red," they begged, "please, please don't hide."

In less than a flash, with more than a rumble,

Lady appeared, or should I say - tumbled.

"Please help us free Nell. Please play us a song.

If you'll play for us, then we'll sing along."

"Jam days and jelly nights," they said.

"Very good on crackers or bread."

Then Lady Red spoke, "You've never been nice.

Why is it that my looks make people look twice?

You really shouldn't stare and sneer,

When you see me, as I come near.

So, if you want some help from me.

Sing to the monster - to set Nell free."

"Jam days and jelly nights," they said.

"We'll sing, while you play, 'til she's free - Lady Red."

Then Red spoke again, "The Monster is lonely.

And, I'm his best friend, but I'm the ONLY.

If he was convinced that someone else cared...

Oh, what's the use, you're much too scared.

Try not to show that you are afraid.

And, don't stop singing while the song is played."

"Jam days and jelly nights," they said.

"We'll sing, while you play, 'til she's free - Lady Red."

So everyone sang songs of love-so-true.

The sky turned purple, red and blue.

The Monster's tail began to whir.

His long pink tail began to stir,

All of the colors of the sky.

And then - fireworks began to fly.

"Jam days and jelly nights," they said.

"Very good on crackers or bread."

Then all of a sudden, everyone looked.

The Monster's tail had Nellie hooked.

The Lady yelled, "Sing loud. Don't stop!"

In one second flat, Nell came to the top.

The meaning of love was clearer than clear -

That ugly's not ugly except for our fear.

"Jam days and jelly nights," they said.

"Love with your heart instead of your head."

Yes, Mean Lady Red made her point crystal clear.
That ugly's not ugly except for our fear.
"Remember," she said "what you saw here tonight.
Or never again see with love's magic light.
It changes and brightens the scariest face,
And gives it such beauty, such style and such grace."

"Jam days and jelly nights," they said.
"We'll never forget what we learned, Lady Red."